Click

Antonique Wickham

ISBN: 9781793312730

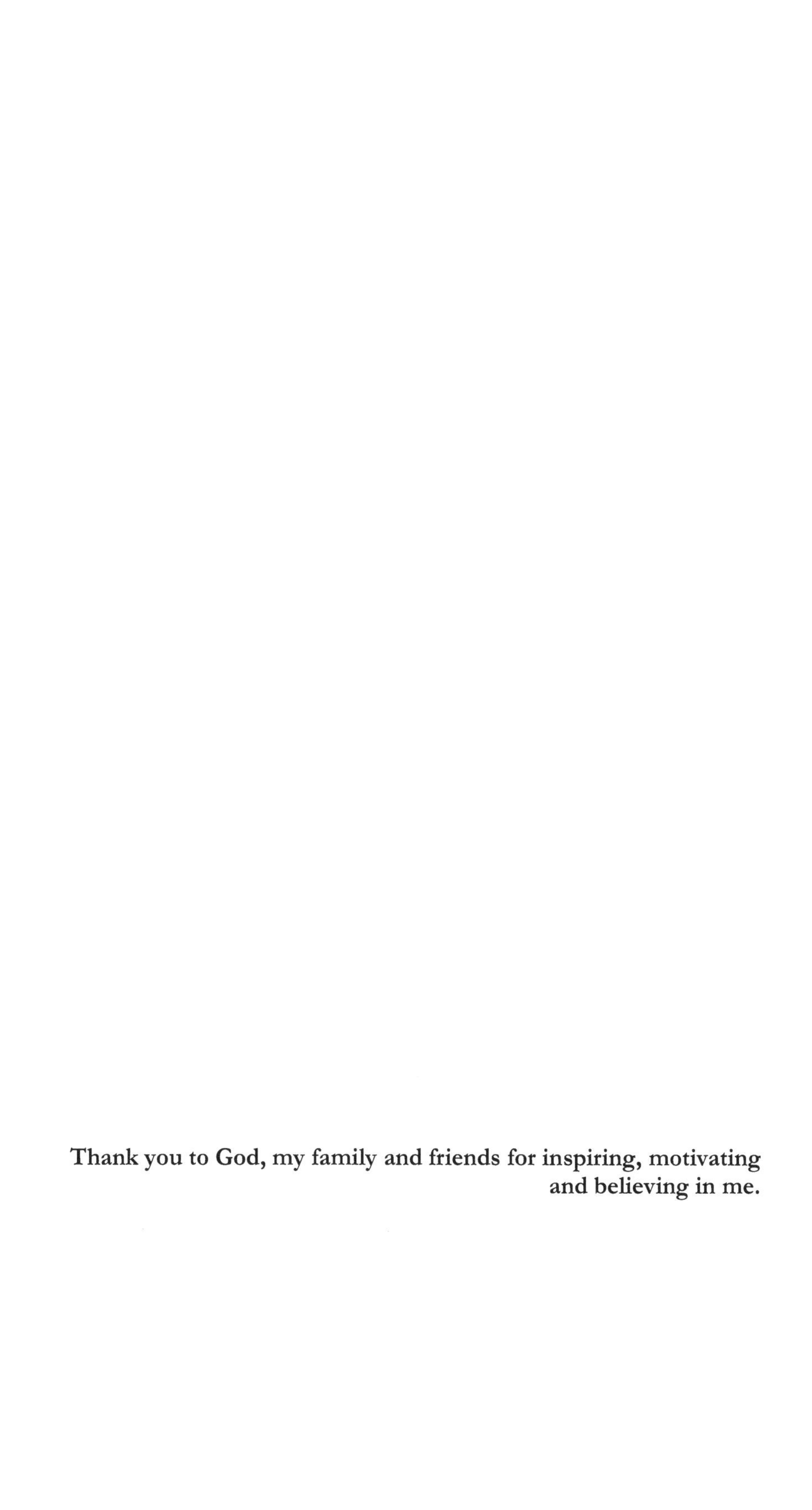

Thank you to God, my family and friends for inspiring, motivating and believing in me.

CONTENTS

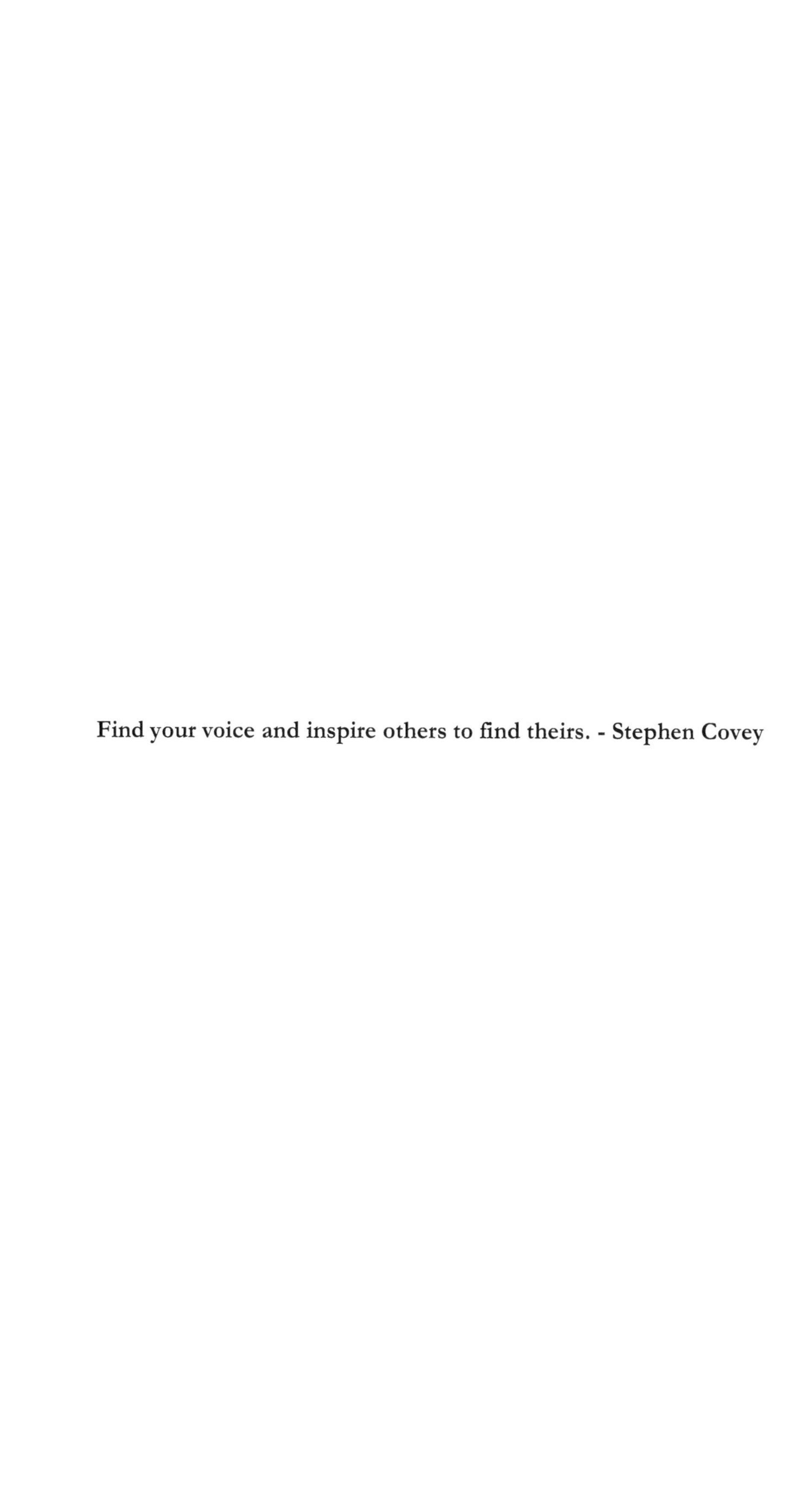

Find your voice and inspire others to find theirs. - Stephen Covey

1

10 HOURS: MICK AND SARAH

"News is now coming in that it has now been official that all persons…"

"Sarah, we need to be ready in five!" Mick called from the garage. His USB stick with all the codes had to be at the bottom of the box. He continued to dig through the box frantically.

"If anyone is found without a Social Media Platform account…"

"Sarah?" Mick knew it was unfair that he had left her to sort out their two children, but he needed to find that USB stick.

"The government officials are ruling that it could be 3 years imprisonment…"

"Got it! … Sarah?" Mick triumphantly lifted the USB stick out of the box marked 'confidential'. He turned the small television off, ran out of the garage into the main part of the house and paused. Elegant pictures decorated the wide corridor showing various family trips in different parts of the country and organized events Mick and Sarah had needed to attend. The black marble floor added an extra shine to the classy images. Mick took a deep breath, taking in the fact that their lives were about to drastically change.

"Mick? Are you ready?" Sarah's voice pulled him out of his trance. Sarah now stood calmly in front of him with a composed look on her face. He rarely saw her without make up and forgot how beautiful she was without it. He remembered when he used to spend his mornings counting the freckles on her olive-tone skin and running his hands through her long, black hair. She was the calm to his storm.

"Sorry…Yeah I am. I found the USB stick," Mick mirrored her soft tone. She had the ability to bring serenity in the midst of an outburst of chaos.

"Good. Children are ready. I'll get them into the car," Sarah placed a hand on Mick's wide shoulder and walked back through the corridor. Mick would follow her wherever she went.

Mick closed his eyes, took a deep breath and then began to do the final checks around the house. When he was satisfied, he walked slowly towards the family laptop. He was unsure whether he was ready to do the final task. He looked at the logo on the website already set up on the screen. Sarah must have already logged in and left the website up for Mick. Keeping his fingers steady, he typed in his username and password and his SMP page opened up before him. The '-50' in bold red lettering reminded him of their predicament and made his next action easier. He led the cursor to the 'My Account' section of the webpage and opened his account details. Without hesitation, he directed the cursor to 'Deactivate Account' and pressed down hard on his mouse. Click.

Mick ran out of the house, locking the door behind him, in case anyone was watching his movements. Just as he stepped onto his drive, his neighbour called out to him from her front garden next door.
"Hey Mick! Where are you all off to today?" the elderly neighbour waved her garden glove in the air, while the other hand held onto a large pair of shears.
"Oh, hi Sandra," Mick looked to his family sitting in the car and then looked back at Sandra. "Well, just a quick trip to the park. Always have to make the most of free time."

"That's true. Life is so busy and now with this new change in currency. It's hard to keep up."

Mick nodded, trying to subtly walk away from the conversation.

Sandra seemed not to notice, "I was admiring the topiary trees Sarah had put at the front of the house."

"Hmmm" Mick, distracted, kept looking back to the car to make sure the family was still safe. "Oh yes. The trees. Tell you what Sandra, you can have them. We weren't too sure about them, so it's best they have a home where they are appreciated."

"Oh I couldn't!" Sandra had already dropped the shears and was making her way towards the top of Mick's drive. "Thank you. I tell you what. I'll give you a like, when I get back in."

"Oh no, you don't have to do that. It's our gift to you. We don't want anything in return," Mick had managed to make his way to the car and had his hand ready to pull the handle.

Sandra lifted one of the topiary trees and began walking towards her house, "Nonsense! I shall do it now! I'm sure you don't need the likes, but it's the least I can do."

Mick hurriedly opened the car door and started the car. He had had the good sense to exchange his Range Rover Evoque for a Toyota Yaris, making it harder for them to be found. Luckily, Sandra hadn't asked about the change of vehicle. Mick quickly reversed the car off the drive and pulled forward onto the main road. He felt Sarah gazing at him.

"We need to get out of here. Fast," was all he could manage to say. He was anxious that at any moment, they could be found and what was most important to them, would all disappear. Sarah nodded in response and looked back at the children.

"Who's ready for an adventure?" Sarah pumped her fists in the air and glanced back at Mick. He wondered if she knew how much he appreciated her in these moments.

"Me!" the children yelled in unison from the back of the car. Craig, their first son, smiled revealing his missing two front teeth. This was a normal look for most eight-year olds, but Craig hadn't lost his teeth the normal way. Being the adventurous soul he was, he attempted a trick on his new mountain bike and found himself quickly making contact with the hard concrete floor. Cara, three years younger than her brother, had been there telling Craig he would be okay. She had that same look now. One of uncertainty but reassurance. Mick often thought she would be more like her mum.

Mick started the small car and took his family on their adventure. There had been rumours of a group living outside of the rule of SMP further north, so they had no other destination but north. The 'Rebel' camp was rumoured to be 200 miles from their city and hidden away from the government officials, who would now be at full force looking for those who hadn't signed up to SMP.

The drive to the camp was smooth. Mick and Sarah had prepared for the worst case scenario, carrying disguises just in case they got pulled over. The family had enjoyed taking the scenic route through the beautiful country lanes. It was different from their life in the city. Every so often they would come across a herd of cottages huddled closely together in their villages. Plants covered the side of most of the cottages, as if the country life was trying to swallow up all of its inhabitants. The picturesque views had kept the children in awe as they saw hills that Craig had cried out were as tall as giants. It was as if the hills stood over them in their green military gear guarding their escape from the city. After a while, Sarah led the children into a number of songs and must have tired them out, as one hour into the journey they had fallen asleep. The rest of the time, Sarah entertained Mick with conversations about what their new non-materialistic life would look like. Fishing in the morning, whilst the sun was making its way into the sky. Swimming in fresh water lakes, enjoying the feel of the water on their 'city-life' skin. Listening to the lullaby of insects and wild animals and sleeping under a blanket of stars. This utopic lifestyle was appealing but Mick wondered if they would be able to sustain it. Eventually, Sarah had ended with, "What are we going to do?"

It was Mick's turn to be the hopeful one. "When we get to the Rebel camp, we can start making plans. We can just take everything one day at a time."

“I know. I’m just so mad at SMP. We’ve had to change our lives. My account was -50 when I deactivated it.”

“Same as mine. Employer dissatisfaction. They have the power to lower our scores. Social Media Platform. How have they now taken over the world?”

“-50,” it was almost as if Sarah didn’t hear Mick, as she continued her rant. “How did they expect us to live off that? We would have lost our home, our jobs…we would not have been able to afford to buy food. A loaf of bread is 10 points. -50 Mick. The world is going mad.”

All Mick could do in response was sigh. “SMP is now the world’s currency Sarah. It is a fact we have to deal with. The more people like you, the more points you have.”

“Well, I’m glad we chose to leave that world behind,” Sarah reached out and touched Mick’s hand. Just with that touch his heart was softened, and any concerns Mick had, melted away.

After about 3 hours, they arrived at the Rebel camp. A secure gate surrounded a huge mansion. How the Rebels had obtained this, Mick had no idea. Before they had planned to leave, Mick had been hearing about a Rebel camp where people wanted to hide away from the pressures of social media. With no support from the government, they would have found it difficult to support a place of this size. He was surprised to now see that this was the place where the Rebels resided. He had expected to see tents, sheep and chickens. They may not have abandoned their life of luxury after all.

Mick pulled up to the gate and saw there was an intercom. Leaving Sarah with the children, he stepped out of the car and rang the buzzer. No response. Mick wasn’t surprised. The whole world had been in disarray when SMP had declared a new way of living. Likes could be converted into currency. Riots had ensued, as opinionated characters shared their thoughts openly and argued with anyone who disagreed. But SMP only had to wait for a culture to be created, to allow for the culture to create a new set of thinkers. The school of thought spread like a disease. Even though the riots had calmed down, anybody against SMP were now a minority so if they spoke against them, they would be attacked. This was why the Rebels had gone into hiding and may have been why they were not answering him. You can never be too careful. Mick rang two more times and waited. After about ten minutes, he walked back to the car.

"No luck?" Sarah asked.

"No. I'm going to find another way in. But I want to make sure you guys are safe, so I'll make sure the car is out of sight."

Mick hid the car under a row of trees and made his way back to the camp. The tall gate had been placed in the middle of a wooden fence and Mick couldn't see no other way in. He carried on walking around the fence, until he noticed a loose panel. He pushed the panel and placed his hand through the gap. This allowed him to pull on the panels standing next to the loose one. When he made a big enough gap, he pushed himself through the hole. He would rebuild the fence, he just needed to make sure his family was safe. After climbing through the hole, he stood in awe of what he saw. Clothes and food were scattered all over the driveway of the mansion. It was like a rainbow had exploded and all the colours had been sprayed across the grass and pebbles. Mick walked slowly towards the mansion. Behind the many windows, he could only see darkness and the door of the building was ajar. The mansion seemed like it would have been majestic and a landmark to all but now it looked pitiful. Mick pulled the front door open and called out. No response. He should have known. Who would hang about to wait for SMP unleash its fury to those who refused to fall in line? The Rebels had probably left in a hurry knowing that this was one of the places SMP would look first. Mick was about to hurry back to the car, when he heard the sound of crashing echo down the corridor.

2

10 HOURS: ZEN AND ELLIE

Zen lay on her bed looking at her phone. She had been staring at her phone for the past fifteen minutes, like she had the mental capacity to change the words laid out on the illuminated screen.

Zen. It's best we don't talk. I'm sorry it's for the best. Liam

At least he was straight to the point, she thought. She had known Liam for a year and loved him for 11 months. She wasn't the type to fall in love quickly, but she had been attracted to his character right from the start. He was intelligent and witty. Playful and wise. Generous and honest. Zen thought it was too good to be true but when he had told her he loved her three months into dating, she knew she wanted to spend the rest of her life with him. So why this text? Why now? Why not say it to her face? Zen went through a range of emotions. Her sadness would overtake her anger and then she would be filled with contempt. In her despair she didn't want to call him or reply to his message. If he truly loved her, he would have had a proper conversation with her. Why relay these things through a text?

After fifteen more minutes, Zen decided the pity party was over and it was time she moved forward. She walked from the bedroom of her small apartment into her open plan living room and switched on the television. The morning news greeted her with the face of a stern woman reading from her script.

"News is now coming in that it has now been official that all persons…"

BUZZZZZZZZ

The sound of the apartment buzzer pulled Zen's attention away from the television. She lifted up the receiver and waited for the person to talk.

"Zen. Its me, Ellie. Let me in please. Its urgent."

"Ahhh. Alright Ellie, but you better be quick. I start work in an hour." Zen put the receiver down and turned back to the television. It's all negative anyway, she thought, and turned the television off.

"Have you been watching the news?" Ellie asked as she walked into the apartment.

"No of course not. All that negativity at the start of my day. No thanks."

"So you don't know what's happening? The SMP are arresting people who have no account. It's compulsory now to have a social media account and likes are the new currency."

Zen laughed, "And this is why I don't watch the news. What a bunch of baloney! They're going to arrest every single person who doesn't conform. That's a lot of people. Likes have always been an option for currency but not the only option."

"Well they said they are, and it seems pretty serious. Three years minimum. They had announced a while back that it was going to become the only currency."

"Sounds like car fines. If you ignore them, they just go away."

"Zen! You'll be taken to court. I hope you haven't been doing that!"

"You sound like my mum! Anyway what are you here for? Remember I need to leave in a bit."

"Oh yeah. Well, I received a letter from my mum."

"Your mum? You haven't heard from her in years," Zen raised her hand signaling for Ellie to sit with her on the sofa in the living room.

"I know. It's been such a long time. But she wrote to tell me, she's going to join the Rebels and asked me to join her."

"Wow! That's a huge decision for her to make. So, what are you going to do?"

"I'm going to join her."

Zen laughed again, "You? If I don't hear from you, I know you're still alive from the hundreds of selfies you post."

"Why hide all of this from the world?" Ellie stood and twirled in the middle of the living room.

Zen rolled her eyes, "Seriously Ellie. If SMP are bad as you say they are, this is a huge decision to make."

"I just feel this calling you know. To follow in the steps of my mum and change the world."

"Fair enough. It will be awesome for you to see her."

"I know right. But anyway. That is not why I came. I wanted you to ask to come with me."

"Me? Why me?"

"You! You're the perfect person. You're the only person I know who has a great disdain for 'the world and all of its systems' as you say. I don't want to make this journey alone and anybody else would be too afraid to lose their like scores. I need a rebel to find a Rebel."

Zen thought about it for a while. "If we go, you will have to go offline. Like no internet. Being a Rebel means going on the run. Like I said, if SMP are as bad you say they are, you don't want them to find you visiting Rebel camps."

"I thought about that. Look I'm making the journey to my mum and I'm prepared to do anything to make it," Ellie looked at Zen defiantly.

"Okay then. How bad is this SMP thing? When does it come into force?"

"Today. They're starting with anyone who hasn't got an account at all and giving them warnings. People will then have seven days to set up their account."

"Wow they're not playing."

"Nope!"

"Well, I think today will have to be the day we leave this world behind. We have to leave now while the numbers are high. Soon there will only be a few people left without accounts and we'll be the first to be caught."

"I thought you would say that! So, I brought my stuff. It's in the car," Ellie smiled at Zen.

"How did you know I would say yes?"

"And pass up an opportunity to defy the government? I know you Zen. I wouldn't be surprised if you told me you were secretly the leader of the Rebels."

Zen giggled, "Okay give me ten minutes to pack my things and then we can go."

Zen made sure she put all essential clothing and food into a back pack, ensuring she had enough clothing should the weather take a turn for the worst. When she had finished packing, she brought her laptop out into the living room and gave it to Ellie.

"Ready to say goodbye to your old life Ellie?"

Ellie grabbed the laptop from Zen. Zen wasn't sure if it was just a façade or if Ellie was actually excited to deactivate her account. Either way, this was a momentous occasion to watch someone who lived and breathed social media. Zen watched as Ellie rapidly found the SMP website and logged into her account. She guided the mouse to the 'My Account' area and hesitated. Suddenly, Ellie found the words, 'Deactivate Account', and then pressed down on the mouse. Click.

Zen and Ellie rushed to Ellie's car and carefully packed Zen's belongings into the boot. Once they were ready, Ellie sat in the driver side and Zen in the passenger. Zen looked down the street where her apartment block stood. Why hadn't she noticed the vacant houses before? She had heard that a small number of families had been leaving the properties over the past six months but didn't think anything of it. At this time of day, she would have been met with laughter from children playing on the street. The deafening silence was new to this street and had gone unnoticed.

"Where is everyone?" Zen thought out loud.

"I've *been* trying to tell you Zen. The world is now do or die. Those who can't live with this new currency have had to go into hiding. Those who can't earn enough likes have had to downsize. I don't know how you would have survived! You're so anti-social, you wouldn't have been able to gain any likes to live!"

Zen pushed Ellie in response, whilst still looking at the deserted street.

"So where did your mum say this Rebel camp is?" Zen pulled out an old map she had had in the house.

"About 100 miles from here. About there," Ellie pointed to a place on the map. "But why don't we just use our phones?"

"You got us going off the grid, Ellie. I'm not trusting any piece of technology for us to get caught."

"True. Okay well, looking at the map it looks like it will take around 2 hours. Usually my phone will tell me the ETA, but since we can't use them…" Ellie rolled her eyes.

"Stop being over-dramatic Ellie. We better get going."

Ellie gave Zen a smile and started the car. It wasn't long before they had driven to the main road and were on their way to their destination. Ellie kept Zen entertained with conversations about what she remembered about her mum when she was a child. About an hour into the journey, Ellie went quiet.

"What's wrong?" Zen looked at Ellie, puzzled.

"Erm…we…the car's low on petrol," Ellie kept both hands firmly on the steering wheel.

"Oh Ellie!" Zen knew she should have checked if Ellie had actually sorted *everything*. Ellie was often making spontaneous plans without thinking about the detail.

"We probably have another 20 miles," Ellie glanced apologetically at Zen.

"That will leave us with just over 30 miles, Ellie. What are we going to do? Walk?" Zen tried to hold back her frustration.

"I don't know. I don't know. I thought it would be enough."

Zen closed her eyes for a few seconds. "Okay. We have to stop somewhere. If we don't, we will have to walk and I'm not sure that that's a safer option."

"Okay. We'll stop at the nearest station and hope they haven't changed their currency."

Ellie continued for another ten miles, until they saw a small petrol station at the side of the road. They pulled in and Zen began to fill up the car. The petrol station was quiet, with one other driver filling up a small convertible. When the tank was full, she returned the petrol pump and walked into the shop area. She had instructed Ellie to stay in case Ellie needed to drive away quickly, leaving Zen if necessary.

“Hi, pump 5 please,” Zen tried to speak confidently to the cashier.

“That’s 20 likes please,” the middle-aged man smiled.

“Oh, are you still not using the old currency?” Zen began to dig around in her purse to avoid eye contact with the cashier.

“That changed today, I’m afraid. Only accepting likes now,” the cashier pointed to a sign that read, ‘LIKES ONLY”.

“Oh, I see. Well my phone died, and I only have old currency on me,” Zen showed the black screen on her phone to the cashier.

“Well, you can charge it here or use my phone to log into your account. But if you don’t pay, I will need to call the police,” the cashier’s pleasant smile had turned into an angry frown.

“No need for that,” responded Zen, thinking carefully about her next move. “If you lend me your charger, I can give you the likes.”

“Perfect. One second,” the cashier bent down below the counter to find the charger. Whilst, his head was down, Zen ran out of the shop and into the car.

“Drive! Drive! Drive!” Zen yelled at Ellie. Ellie quickly put the car into gear and drove onto the main road, just in time to see the cashier running behind them. He couldn’t keep up and it wasn’t long before he and the petrol station was a speck in the distance.

“You did it!” Ellie smiled, relieved.

“And I don’t want to do it again!” Zen laughed, lying back in the passenger seat.

After some time, the map directed them off the main road. The country lane was surrounded by beautiful sights of tall hills and majestic fields. The country lane soon became narrow and then ended with a metal gate. Ellie and Zen jumped out of the car and looked ahead. They had seemingly stopped in front of a vast, green field. In the distance they could make out the shape of a tall building.

"You think that's it?" Ellie asked Zen.

"Yeah, we better get going and leave the car here. It should be fine."

Ellie and Zen steadily climbed over the metal gate and walked through the field. Thirty minutes later they arrived at the building they had seen when they first got out of the car. In front of them, stood a tall a wooden fence hiding the Rebel camp from prying eyes. The fence, about twice their height, looked like it had been built in a hurry.

"How are we going to get in?" Zen asked. "Did your mum leave any instructions?"

"She wrote the letter on her way here. She didn't say how to get in. There has to be an entrance around here somewhere."

Ellie and Zen walked around the fencing until they got to a tall gate. Zen walked up to the intercom and pressed the buzzer. Silence. Zen pressed the buzzer again after about a minute. Silence.

"Maybe nobody's home?" Ellie shrugged her shoulders.

"Or… news of the SMP has sent everyone further into hiding," Zen tried to peer through the gate. "It looks like a beautiful building though."

"Mmm. Well there's only one way to find out," Ellie started looking for another entrance into the camp.

"There's two of us. How about you give me a lift?"

Ellie's eye glanced over the height of the fence. "Okay, let's try. But how will I get over?"

"We'll take off our jackets and create a type of rope. What do you think?"

"And our t-shirts. We can still try though."

Zen placed one of her feet into Ellie's cupped hands and reached for the top of the fence. She pulled herself to the top and rolled over to the other side of the fence and dropped down. Moments later, Ellie threw their make shift rope over the fence. Zen held onto the other side of the material, while she felt Ellie's weight pull on the other side. Once Ellie had climbed the height of the fence, she turned herself around and jumped down. By then, Zen had moved to the side and had turned to look at the Rebel building.

"Zen? Zen?" Ellie followed Zen's gaze and saw what she was looking at. Food and clothes were scattered all over the driveway, distracting the view of the mansion. The mansion itself was huge, with a number of decrepit windows, with a row at the top and a row at the bottom. It was as if the mansion was smiling at them with its crooked teeth.

"What do you think happened?" Ellie looked around the littered premises, whilst putting her t-shirt and jacket back on.

"It looks like they left in a rush but why is everything everywhere?"

"Look the door has been left open," Ellie pointed towards the faded, archaic door.

Ellie and Zen walked slowly towards the mansion. Zen pulled the door of the mansion and cautiously walked inside.

"Hello?" Zen called out, as Ellie walked behind her. Her voice echoed around the empty building. In front of them, marble stairs spiraled to the top of the mansion. They were standing in the middle of a wide corridor that stretched either side of them, with rooms coming off the corridor like fingers.

"Let's look in some of these rooms. We might be able to find supplies," Ellie pulled Zen towards the corridor to the left. The first room they came to was the kitchen. It was just as cluttered as the driveway. Pots, pans and mixing bowls had seemingly been flung around the massive kitchen. Suddenly, they heard the close of a door. Ellie and Zen stopped in their tracks and looked at each other. Zen grabbed Ellie's hand and pulled her down behind the kitchen unit in the middle of the room. As Ellie ducked down, her elbow knocked a mixing bowl that had been hanging over the side. The mixing bowl fell to the floor with a softened thump but the utensils that were in the mixing bowl clattered onto the ground. Ellie and Zen crouched down further, as they heard footsteps coming towards them.

3

14 HOURS

Mick walked down the corridor until he arrived at the first room. It looked like it was the kitchen, but the room was in such disarray with bowls and food everywhere. Plastic bags and more bowls covered the floor. The culprit of the crashing seemed to lie to the right of the middle unit. The utensils lay scattered on the floor. Mick walked over to the unit to pick up the utensils, when something caught his eye.

"Who are you?" Mick stepped back from the utensils.

Ellie and Zen stood up slowly.

"I'm Ellie and this is Zen. Who are you? Are you a government official?"

"No, I…I'm looking for the Rebel camp," Mick looked at Ellie and Zen wearily. It was hard to know who to trust.

"So are we!" Ellie jumped in excitement. "He's looking for the Rebel camp too, Zen!"

"I heard," Zen gave Ellie a stern look and pulled her to the side. "How do you know he's being honest?"

Ellie shrugged her shoulders and looked back over at Mick. "We might not have a choice but to trust him."

"Sorry, what was your name?" Zen turned back round to face Mick.

"Mick. I'm Mick. Look. I was hoping to find the Rebel camp here and obviously all the Rebels are gone. So I'm going to head over to the next camp."

"Another camp?" Ellie looked at Mick questioningly.

"Yeah. North of here, there is another camp. I'm going to go out on a limb here and say that you two are not government officials. You are more than welcome to join me and my family," Mick questioned whether he had made the right decision but hoped that his kindness would go a long way.

"And how do you know about this camp, Mick? How can we trust you?" Zen looked Mick up and down. He looked like the business type, with his short, black hair combed back into a slick style. He was clean-shaven and seemed as if he always carried a serious look on his face. He had obviously traded his suit for a t-shirt, jeans and a bomber jacket, as he didn't seem comfortable in his casual attire. Zen wondered what would make a man go off the grid with his family.

"You don't have to. But I have to go back to my family. I don't want to be driving around with my family when it's dark," Mick placed his hands in his pocket and waited for either Ellie or Zen respond.

"Okay, we'll come. Let's just look for any supplies we can find and then go," Ellie looked at Zen reassuringly. Surely, he wasn't a government official. Why would he be travelling with his family?

Ellie, Zen and Mick hurriedly looked around for any food they could find in the kitchen. There were only a few tins left and with no back pack, the trio had to carry what they could in their hands. When they had finished searching the kitchen, Mick, Ellie and Zen made their way back out of the mansion to the tall fence. Mick showed Ellie and Zen the entrance he had created and led them out back into the field. Mick agreed to meet Ellie and Zen where they had parked, after they had explained how to get there. Ellie and Zen travelled back to their car and waited for Mick to arrive. Mick travelled back to his car and hoped Sarah wouldn't flip. Mick walked back to the car and saw that Sarah and the children were fast asleep. He quietly climbed into the car and nudged Sarah.

"Oh you're back. Did you see anyone?" Sarah placed her head on Mick's shoulder.

"Well, all the Rebels are gone. I'm not surprised because this is probably one of the first places SMP will come to. Just thought maybe we could have caught up to the Rebels before they left. But, there were also two ladies there in the same predicament as us," Mick looked at Sarah and tried to gage her expression.

"Are they also Rebels?" Sarah took her head off Mick's shoulder.

"They're going off the grid as well. I told them that they can follow us to the camp further North."

Sarah raised her eyebrows. Would these strangers jeopardise their low profile?

"It should be fine," Mick rubbed Sarah's hand. "Somehow I think it will help if we're more trusting."

"As long as we trust the right people," Sarah and Mick said in unison. Sarah held onto Mick's hand.

"You're always good at reading people. I trust your judgment call," Sarah looked at Mick in the eye and Mick raised his eyebrows. "We just read one person wrongly, that's all," Sarah placed her head back on Mick's shoulder.

Mick paused to take in the moment. He often wondered where he would be without Sarah and particularly in this situation, Mick was especially thankful for her. After a few minutes, Mick started the car and drove around to where Ellie and Zen were parked. Mick drove through the country lane, until it became narrow and saw another vehicle as he was nearing the dead end. He parked behind the car and he and Sarah climbed out of the car. Mick led Sarah to the car and waited for Ellie and Zen to greet them.

When Ellie and Zen saw Mick and Sarah approach the car, they both climbed out of the car and went to meet Sarah.

"Hi, I'm Zen and this is Ellie. Nice to meet you."

"Hi, I'm Sarah," Sarah shook both Ellie's and Zen's hands. "Sorry if I seem quite hesitant but we also have our children with us. Can't afford to make friends with the wrong people." Ellie and Zen nodded in agreement. "So what's your story?"

"Well, I asked Zen to help me look for my mum. She has become a Rebel."

"Oh wow," Sarah seemed to relax more at the mention of the word 'Rebel'.
"And what about you guys? We didn't get time to ask at the mansion," Sarah looked at the girl who had just posed the question and tried to remember her name. Zen. Her long, black hair was tied up like she was ready to go to war, whereas her friend Ellie seemed more relaxed as she had allowed her brown, curly hair to hang down onto her shoulders.

"Well, we didn't want our children growing up in this world," Mick held onto Sarah's hand.

"We were in the corporate world," Sarah added. "SMP not only affected our work life but our home life, so we had to get out."

"We understand," Zen looked at Mick and Sarah more sympathetically. She had misjudged them.

"So where is the other Rebel camp?" Ellie asked.

"Right," Mick pulled out a map from his car and flattened it out on the bonnet of his car. "My sources said there was one around here," Mick pointed to a space of greenery on the map.

"How long do you think it will take?" Zen also didn't want to be travelling at night.

“Err…another 200 miles. We’ll be there before dark, if we head straight there. But we will also need to stop for more petrol.”

“We will too,” Ellie looked over at Zen.

“It should be fine,” Mick reassured Ellie. “It’s quieter in the countryside so no one will be trying to check our identities and most places are still using the old currency.”

“What if someone wants to give us a like?” Ellie was twiddling her thumbs nervously.

“Or an unlike,” Mick laughed but his joke was met with grim faces. “Okay. Well, we can just say that our accounts are down.”

“I guess that can work,” Ellie stopped twiddling her thumbs.

“Okay, so we better get going. Stay close behind. If anything happens, just keep heading north,” Mick said.

Mick, Sarah, Ellie and Zen all exchanged numbers in case of an emergency and got back into their cars. Mick drove back onto the main country lane and headed north. They were able to get petrol at the nearest petrol station without any trouble, as they explained to the cashier that they needed to get rid of the old currency. Luckily, nobody wanted to give them likes or unlikes and so the group were able to travel north undetected. Four hours later, they arrived at what had been the green space on the map.

Mick stopped the car and climbed out to investigate where the map had led them to. In front of him stood a dilapidated wooden cabin. Wooden panels were falling from the cabin, as if they were trying to escape from the derelict structure. Wet moss crept up the sides of the cabin and the door hung wide open hanging off its hinges. The small windows seemed to be squinting at him as the wooden window frames sloped down at an angle. Mick hadn’t noticed Ellie and Zen standing by his side, while he was staring at the wooden construction.

“Why here?” Zen’s voice pulled Mick out of his trance.

"I…It must have been a mistake," Mick looked at the cabin in disbelief.

"We followed the map. It might have been one of the original hideouts but it's clear no one lives here," Ellie looked her watch. "It's 5pm. Shall we keep looking for another camp?"

Mick placed his hands in his pocket, "Let me look around here first. It's going to be dark soon so the sooner we find a place to stay, the better."

Mick left Ellie and Zen standing by the cars and walked towards the cabin. The two steps leading up to the collapsing door had missing panels, so Mick tried to walk up the steps carefully. The rickety door groaned loudly, as Mick pushed it into the dusty, deserted cabin. Inside, there was hardly any light due to the small windows. Mick took out his phone from his pocket and shone the torch. The light revealed that the cabin consisted of one room with just a table and chair in the middle. Mick placed his fingers on his temples, dragged his hands down to his chin and held them there for a few seconds. This may have to be their shelter for the night. Although the cabin was crumbling on the outside, the wooden beams inside seemed sturdy enough to stop the archaic structure from falling on top of their heads whilst they slept. Mick placed his hands into his pockets and walked back outside. By now, the children were outside of the cars, running around the vehicles playing a game of tag and Sarah was talking to Ellie and Zen.

"What was it like?" Sarah asked when she noticed Mick walking towards them.

"It can work," Mick rubbed his chin thoughtfully. "We carried enough blankets, so we can use them to sleep on the floor. I'm just worried that it will be dark soon and we may carry on looking and find nothing better than this. Better we rest and look further tomorrow."

"Okay. A little camping didn't hurt anybody. Let's get everything sorted," Sarah placed her hand on Mick's shoulder and then walked back towards the car.

4

72 HOURS

The group had spent two nights at the cabin. Not because they enjoyed their new luxury accommodation, but Mick had stressed the importance of staying until they had formulated a plan. Just travelling north was too vague when their well-being was at stake. They had spent the night sleeping on blankets, with one person on look-out for a couple of hours. The days, the children spent playing in their new surroundings and the adults spent discussing the new plan of action. Food consisted of fruit for breakfast, cold, canned goods for lunch and hot, canned goods for dinner after Mick had built a fire. It certainly was a world away from what Mick and Sarah were used to, but it was better than nothing.

It was the evening of the third day when the group finally settled on a decision.

"Maybe we should stay here," Ellie said, finishing her can of hot spaghetti hoops.

"But what about the Rebels? What about your mum?" Zen looked at Ellie confused.

"I want to find her, but it's too easy to get caught at the moment. We're living rough, but it's better than nothing. Maybe it's better to wait until things have calmed down," Ellie placed her hand on Zen's arm reassuringly. "They've probably already searched the mansion to find the Rebels had already escaped. I doubt they will come here because it doesn't look like anyone in their right mind would live here." The rest of the group smiled. "Anywhere we try and go now, the SMP will be looking. Wait until things calm." Zen sensed that Ellie had finally come to understand the predicament they were in and fear oozed from her strong speech.

"What do you think?" Zen asked turning to Mick and Sarah.

"I think Ellie may have a point. But I wouldn't want to stay here too long. We're just sitting ducks. Let's give it a few more days. Things should have calmed down by then and the SMP won't be looking for the Rebels so aggressively," Mick gave Ellie a smile of support. He had sensed the fear too.

"Okay sorted. Kids help me tidy up," Sarah called out to Craig and Cara, who were happily playing a game of cards in the corner of the room.

"I'm just going to get something from the car," Zen walked out towards the two vehicles, which had been hidden behind the trees. Brushing off leaves and branches, Zen climbed into the car and took out her bag. Anything that wasn't necessary was kept in the cars, as the cabin could just about allow all 6 of them to sleep in there. Zen carefully pulled out a picture of her and Liam from the front of the backpack. He had been her family for the past year and that's why his text message had hurt so much more. She had never known her parents and couldn't wait to get away from her adopted parents as soon as she turned 18. Besides Ellie, Liam had been the closest person to her. She held onto the photograph, then decided to go for a walk. After carefully placing the branches and leaves back onto the car, Zen walked a few meters deeper into the woods. Suddenly she heard the crunching of leaves coming from in front her. Without hesitating, Zen began to climb the tree in front of her. Within minutes, she had reached the top and had a better vantage point of what had caused the noise. Beneath her she could see two people walking through the woods, walking towards the cabin. Peering down, she could make out that it was Mick and Sarah. They must have started to walk a full circle around the cabin, after she had left. As she was about to climb down, she heard the hushed voices mention her name.

"Zen will figure us out soon enough. She keeps asking questions about the work we did. It won't be long until she works out the company we worked for," Zen worked out that the voice she was hearing was Sarah's.

"I know. But what do we do? If we tell them, it will only make things worse," Mick was failing to turn his deep voice into a quiet whisper. Mick and Sarah had now stopped walking and were stood a few yards from where Zen was hiding.

"Exactly. We can't just tell them we were the leaders of the SMP!" Sarah was successfully speaking in a quiet tone, but Zen could not mistake what she had heard. She almost fell from the branch she was sitting on.

"I don't think we can. The moment we can no longer keep up the lies, we make up something about having to part ways. Deal?" Mick looked at Sarah, waiting for her to answer.

"Deal," Sarah nodded and led Mick back to the cabin.

Zen waited a few minutes before climbing down the tree. Mick and Sarah were the leaders of the SMP. They had caused all of this. So why were they running away from it? Unless they were trying to track down the Rebels and inform the government officials of their whereabouts. Zen marched back to the cabin, intent on finding out the truth.

When Zen arrived at the cabin, Sarah was getting the children ready to sleep and Mick and Ellie were looking at the map. Everyone turned to face her when she walked into the room.

"Where have you been?" Mick asked. "We thought you might had fallen asleep in the car. You can be on first watch then, as you'll have the most energy."

"I think *you* better tell us the truth," Zen placed her hands firmly on her hips. Ellie looked at Zen confused.

"What are you talking about?" Sarah asked now clutching onto the children.

"Next time you have a private conversation, you need to make sure no-one is around. So, when are you going to let the government officials know about our whereabouts?"

Ellie walked over to Zen and placed her hands on her shoulders, "You should calm down."

"Ellie, we don't know these people. Well, I do know they were the leaders of SMP," Zen looked from Mick to Sarah with disgust.

Ellie took her hands from Zen's shoulders and turned to face Mick and Sarah, "Is this true? Were you using us to get to the Rebels?"

"Yes…No…We…You have to let us explain," Mick hung his head down. "If you come and sit down, we can explain."

Ellie looked at Zen, "We should listen to what they have to say. If they have informed the government officials already, we'll have no chance of getting away anyway."

"We aren't informers," Sarah insisted. "Just…let us explain."

Ellie and Zen walked slowly to Mick and the three of them sat down on the blankets by the side of the room, whilst waiting for Sarah to calm the children down and settle them down for sleep. After 5 minutes, Sarah joined the circle of distrust and began telling Ellie and Zen their story.

Sarah explained that they had in fact been the leaders of SMP. Mick and Sarah's vision of SMP was that it would not only be used to share people's pictures, but that people could trade their likes for anything they needed. They didn't intend for it to become currency, or compulsory. Mick and Sarah had created it together alongside one of Mick's university friends, Josh. About five years after creating SMP, Josh had presented them with the idea of likes being used for currency. Mick and Sarah hated the idea, but unbeknown to them, Josh had already sold the idea to the board and a number of investors. So, when it came for the decision to be made and Mick and

Sarah disagreed, they were ousted. But not before they heard the reasoning behind Josh's plan. SMP being made compulsory allowed the government to not only monitor everything, but also to create cultures. They could decide what was popular and what was not. Pay a few people to give more likes to a certain fad and everyone would go for it. Pay a few people to give 'unlikes' to a disapproving trend, that craze disappears. It could also be done with people. People running for government could soon find their scores in the minus on the SMP, if the 'powers that be' didn't like them - no matter how kind-hearted those people were. If it didn't fit in with the views of the hierarchical social club, it was dismissed. Sarah explained that that was what happened to her and Mick. They had no choice but to go into hiding.

"That's awful," Zen eventually said, when she had processed everything that had been said to her. "So if you disagree, that's the end of you?"

"I'm afraid so," Mick said holding Sarah's hand. "It's a democratic way of running a dictatorship. Make the people think it's what they want. What kind of world is that for our children?"

Everyone looked at the children, who were by now fast asleep. What kind of world would they be living in?

"We're sorry we didn't tell you the truth," Sarah looked remorseful. "If people know we created the SMP, they won't see the fact that we left. They will just see that we created this monster. Even hiding with the Rebels was a risk, but we were willing to take it."

"What would you have done if they recognized that you were the leaders of SMP?" Ellie asked.

"We would have tried to explain ourselves," Mick answered. "That's all we can do now. Live in regret about something we created."

"Why?" Zen stood as she asked.

"Why what?" Sarah asked what everyone else was thinking.

"Why live in regret? Surely, we can do something about it," Zen seemed to be lost in thought.

"We?" Ellie interjected.

Zen carried on as if she hadn't heard Ellie and began pacing the room, "You both created SMP, so that means you know how to take it down. And we have to take it down. We can't go into hiding, while others are being forced to conform to a world they are oblivious to."

"They could go into hiding too," Ellie offered.

"Not everyone thinks that way," Zen responded. "I think we need to take down SMP."

Mick and Sarah sat there stunned. This was not the reaction they had expected.

"Going against SMP. You don't think we tried," Sarah stood this time so she could get Zen's full attention.

"I don't doubt that you did. But I reckon you did whilst trying to hold onto the basics of SMP. You have to get rid of it altogether," Zen placed her hands on her hips.

"She's right," Mick stood next to Sarah. "We can't run away knowing that millions of people will be going through what we went through. Banished if they disagreed with the opinions of the powers that be. No access to food or other necessities. People will die as a result."

"But…how do we?" Sarah looked at Mick questioningly. Surely this was too big for them to handle.

"My USB. I had been working on a code. I just didn't get the opportunity to use it. The code will erase everything SMP from all systems," Mick placed his hands on Sarah's shoulders.

"But someone will just create it again. Something like it," Sarah spoke softer now.

“And that’s why we expose SMP. And who better to do it than the creators!” This time Ellie stood, her face glowing with excitement.

“Oh look who’s excited now to rebel against ‘the world and all its systems’,” Zen raised an eyebrow at Ellie.

“I started this journey so I could find my mum. She decided she wanted to be a Rebel because she must have been able to see all this,” Ellie waved her hands in the air. “If my mum had the opportunity, I think she would fight against SMP. Once we take SMP down, it will be easier to find her, too. She wouldn’t have to be in hiding.” Ellie looked at the others hopeful that everyone was in agreement.

“Well, seems like our plans have changed. I guess we are fighting against the SMP?” Mick asked knowing what the answer was going to be.

“Agreed,” Sarah, Ellie and Zen said in unison.

“Okay. It’s really late now, so I suggest we get some sleep and make a plan first thing in the morning,” Mick said.

5

80 HOURS

The sound of the helicopter echoed throughout the cold, wooden cabin. It had woken everyone up but no one said a word, afraid that even breathing too loud would notify the world of their existence. After a few seconds the noise stopped, but still everyone held their breaths.

"It's gone," sighed Mick after a few minutes.

"We can't stay here," whispered Sarah, clutching Craig and Cara. She had immediately gone to them when the sound of the blades shook the cabin. She could feel the children trembling in her arms.

Ellie and Zen shared a quick glance.

"We'll go and see if we can find somewhere else for us to hide," Zen stood from her make shift bed.

"By yourselves?" Sarah looked at Mick anxiously.

Mick looked at Sarah reassuringly, "They're right Sarah. If they have men on the ground, this is one of the places they will come to first. I can't leave you and the kids here unprotected."

Ellie walked over to Sarah and clasped her hand. "Don't worry, we'll be fine. And we'll be back before dark."

Sarah let go of her children and gave Ellie a hug. "Be safe."

After half an hour, Ellie and Zen had ensured they only had the supplies they needed. Their new venture took them further north.

North meant they would find a safer location, but it also meant that they were away from the supplies they needed in the city. They made sure they discreetly marked their path, so they could find their way back to the cabin. Trying to conserve as much energy as possible, they journeyed in silence.

The sound of the wind tickling the autumn leaves disguised the snapping of twigs beneath their feet. An hour into the journey, it felt as if they were chasing the sun, as its warm rays bounced off their skin. Another hour later and it was time for a rest. Ellie and Zen opened their back packs and quietly looked through the supplies. Ellie pulled out an orange and Zen pulled out a breakfast bar. They soon would not be able to enjoy these luxuries. When they had both finished eating, they placed all their rubbish into their bags and set off again.

The sun began to hang high in the middle of the sky, signifying hope of the group finding safer shelter. Suddenly, Ellie heard a twig snap. She grabbed Zen's arm and pulled her behind a tree. Zen looked at Ellie quizzingly. Ellie tried to signal with her eyes where she heard the sound come from. They waited for a few minutes, hoping to see signs of a wild animal. Nothing. Just as they were about to continue, another twig snapped. This time it was a few yards in front of them.

Ellie and Zen ducked down further behind the tree, as if it was possible for the ground to swallow them up.

"Hi there," a male voice called out.

Ellie and Zen remained still, as if frozen by time.

"I know someone's there. Who are you?" The soft-spoken man seemed to be walking away from them now, as the voice sounded more distant.

"Are you one of us? A Rebel?" The man had changed direction and was walking back towards them.

Zen watched as the fear and horror plastered on Ellie's face molded into excitement. Zen shook her head rapidly, whilst Ellie's eyes pleaded with Zen for them to come out of hiding. They had never met another Rebel before.

"We're here looking for others to help and we've got a shelter not too far from here," the man said softly.

At the mention of 'shelter', Zen had put her hand out to stop Ellie, but she was too late. Ellie had exposed where they had been hiding.

"Hi! I'm Ellie and this is my friend Zen," Ellie grabbed the arm Zen held out and pulled her friend out from behind the tree. Not too far from them stood a tall man with messy brown hair. However, he was oddly clean-shaven telling the girls he must have found a decent shelter to hide away in. His clothes and boots were clean, and his brown eyes declared his innocence.

"I'm Tom," the man waved pleasantly.

Ellie took Zen's hand and walked her closer to Tom.

"We've never met another Rebel," Ellie could hardly contain her excitement.

"These days, we are harder to come by," once they were closer, Tom shook both of their hands.

"I live in a shelter a mile away. We can catch up there," Tom led Ellie and Zen further north and told them about how he had come to be a Rebel. How he was an accountant but soon found the job harder to manage when the company attached itself to the Social Media Platform. Like many others, performance began to be linked to likes, comments and followers. An incident outside of work could cause you to lose a number of clients. Tom explained that, just like many other Rebels, his family had been scared to remain in contact with him, in case they would be imprisoned too. Half an hour later, they had arrived at an abandoned farm. Tom had said that he didn't live in the house because it was the most obvious place anyone would go looking so he had moved into the barn.

The inside of the barn had a nice set up. Tom had moved a set of table and chairs from the house into the barn, alongside a mattress and blankets.

"Where's everyone else?" Zen asked unsettled, once Tom had given the grand tour.

"Another five miles away," Tom's smile seemed to be more sinister or was it the lack of lighting in the barn? "We set up different stations so we can scout, hunt food, find others and protect our group."

"That's a great idea," Ellie set down her back pack and looked around. "There's also more of us. We're actually looking for a place where we can all stay."

Zen shot Ellie a look. Why was she so trusting of this man?

"Oh," a million and one thoughts seemed to be going through Tom's mind. "It would be safer for them to be with the main group of Rebels so they can learn how they live."

"They?" Zen looked from Tom to the exit. When had Tom come between them and the barn door?

"They as in the main group of Rebels," Tom turned to put the locks on the barn door. "We can't be too careful. Surveillance has increased." Tom offered Ellie and Zen a tin of cold soup each and proceeded to tell them about his current scouting mission and all the animals he had come across. Zen thought it was odd that he hadn't asked anything about them.

After an hour or so, Zen stood to pick her up her back pack.

"Thank you, Tom, for your hospitality. We need to head back to our group before dark. We can bring them here and you can show us to the rest of the Rebel group." Zen picked up Ellie's bag and passed it to her.

Tom slowly put his empty can down and walked calmly towards the door.

"I'm afraid I can't do that," the sinister smile that Zen had seen earlier was now spread across Tom's face.

"Don't worry about us," Ellie had been oblivious to Tom's movements whilst adjusting the straps on her back pack. "We know our way back."

Zen had instinctively gone to fish for the pen knife she always kept hidden in her bag.

"I suggest you put your bags down and sit down. Hands off the bag!" The softly spoken Tom was now an aggressive creature with his brown eyes bulging out of his head. He pulled out a long kitchen knife from behind his back and held it out to them. Zen was trying to work out when he had picked up the knife.

Zen put the bag down, not without slipping the pen knife into her pocket. She calmly walked over to Ellie and held her hand. She was sure Ellie hadn't taken another breath yet.

"What do you want, Tom?" Zen clutched onto Ellie's hand.

"Stupid rebels!" Tom laughed to himself. "The very thing you're running from could have saved your life. You would have seen my face plastered all over news feeds. 'WANTED: Man for kidnap and murder'. You don't think it's strange that surveillance has increased around here."

Tom walked closer towards them with the knife. Zen allowed a tear to fall slowly down her cheek, but then squared her shoulders. By now, Ellie's sobs were louder than Zen's racing heart. Zen leant over to Ellie, kissed her on the cheek and whispered, "When the time comes, run."

"Separate now!" Tom waved the knife around in a frenzy.

Zen released Ellie's hand and calmly walked over to the wall of the barn. Tom strode over to Ellie and allowed his finger to glide down her soft, wet cheek.

"Don't worry. It will all be over soon."

"Hands off her!" Tom looked over to see Zen walking towards him with the pen knife. A huge laugh erupted from Tom's tall frame and filled the barn. As if awoken by his joy, Ellie lifted her head up and attempted to slap the knife out of his hand. Her attempt was futile and in retaliation, he slapped her down with his free hand and jumped on top of her.

Tom pointed his knife at Ellie then at Zen yelling, "Come closer and she's dead!" Spittle flew out his mouth and across the room. Zen held his stare for a few more seconds and then dropped her hands by her side.

"Now, throw that pathetic thing over to me. What was you going to do with it, eh? Poke and prod me with it?" This time the eruption of laughter brought Tom rolling off Ellie onto the floor.

Zen took her chance and put the pen knife into her pocket. After a few seconds, Tom stood up and composed himself.

"I said, throw it to me!" he walked closer to Zen and stopped at a safe distance.

Zen slowly took the pen knife out of her pocket and threw it. The pen knife flew out of her hand, over Tom's head and at Ellie's feet. The anger in Tom's face masked the innocence and friendliness he was able to wear before. Without hesitation, he grabbed Zen by the neck and threw her down to the floor.

"Run!" Zen gasped whilst fighting to breathe.

Ellie scrambled for the pen knife and ran over to the locks. The first bolt she undid with ease but the second lock was jammed. As Ellie pulled on the rusty lock, she could hear Tom graphically explaining to

Zen how he was going to end her life. Ellie let out a whimper and before she could pull on the bolt a fifth time, Tom bolted towards her. He grabbed her by the neck and pushed her against the barn door.

"What the hell do you think you are doing?" he spat out at her. "You and your little friend will be dead in seconds. No one will hear you. No one will come looking for you. No one will care. No one will…"

SMASH!

Tom's body lay in a crumpled heap on the floor. Zen had picked up one of the chairs and hit it over the back of his head. Ellie stood there in shock. Pieces of the fragmented, wooden chair lay scattered on the floor.

"Come on Ellie! Help me with the lock."

Ellie ran over to Zen who was already trying to unbolt the door. Between the two of them, they managed to move the bolt and push the barn door open. Zen heard groaning sounds coming from Tom's crumpled body.

"We have to leave the bags! Come on!" she grabbed Ellie's hand and they both raced back through the woods. The sun had not yet set and was providing them with some light to see their way home. After 20 minutes, the sprint they had started off with became a jog.

"We stopped marking our path when we met Tom," Ellie cried breathlessly.

"You did," Zen replied. "I didn't trust him. This way."

By time the sun had completely set, Zen and Ellie had made it back to the cabin. From a distance they could see men swarming the cabin with torches.

"Government officials," Ellie whispered. "What should we do?"

"I don't know," Zen replied defeated.

Zen and Ellie watched the cabin for another ten minutes and saw no sign of Mick, Sarah or the children.

"I think they've taken them," Ellie whispered.

"I think so," Zen began to cry.

"Don't worry. They might have escaped."

"We also have to deal with the fact that Tom will be coming after us."

"So what do we do? Run to the safety of the officials? The same people who should be helping us, could be the ones to bring us the most harm."

Zen dropped her head and rubbed her temples. The dilemma was too much. If Tom found them they were dead. Zen knew they had no choice. They would have to give themselves over to a world they didn't want to fit into.

"Ellie, we're going to need their help." Zen grabbed Ellie's hand, stepped out from behind the tree and slowly walked towards the cabin. An official who had been wandering about a hundred yards from the cabin must have heard the rustling from behind the trees because he stopped dead in his tracks. Zen and Ellie stood still as the official's torch made its way towards them. They instinctively held their hands up as the torch illuminated their location. As quick as the light had exposed their whereabouts it disappeared. Zen and Ellie stood there confused. They watched as the official toyed with the torch in his hand and slowly walked over to where they were. He quickly and quietly grabbed Zen by the hand and pulled her back behind the tree she had hidden behind. Ellie instinctively followed.

"Zen. What are you doing here?"

Zen recognised the hand that held her. How could she not remember the way her hand fit into his? She didn't have to look up to know that his dark brown eyes were taking her in. She heard his conflict each time he took a breath – like he had forgotten how to breathe in her presence.

"Liam. What are you doing here?" Zen couldn't mask the fear in her voice. Just because he once loved her, it didn't mean he wouldn't soon become her captor.

6

82 HOURS

Mick could tell that Sarah was worried about Zen and Ellie wandering the woods on their own. He tried to remind her that when he had met them they were on their own and were surviving okay so they should be fine. Mick could tell by the look on Sarah's face that she was not reassured. She continued to overly fuss over the children like some how they would make up for Zen and Ellie not being there. This was Sarah's way. When they had been working on SMP, she had treated their team the same. Her supportive, nurturing nature gleaming through the darkest days, when team members had had really hard days.

Around midday, a few hours after Ellie and Zen had not returned, even Mick began to get anxious. Although there were no signs of the mysterious helicopter and the sun was still shimmering, Mick had a feeling that something was wrong. He had the same feeling when Josh walked into his office excited that he had been working on something new for SMP. When Mick had asked him what impact these new changes would have on their customers, Josh's smile had become ominous. He had pulled out a document from his back pocket and slapped it down on Mick's desk.

"This! This," he had whispered, "is on a need to know basis."

"Need to know? You, me AND Sarah are the owners of the company. We should already know," Mick had held Josh's stare.

"I know...I know," Josh had actually seemed remorseful, "but I wasn't sure how you were going react. We weren't sure."

There was the return of that smile, Mick thought. Then he registered what Josh had said. "We? Who's we?"

"Okay. Mick." Deep breath. "I've already sold the idea to the board and our investors. Don't give me that look! They thought it was an excellent idea. They even said that if we put it in the right hands, we could push the right political agendas."

"What have you done Josh?"

"Mick! Don't you see the future of SMP? What we can become? A whole ..."

"A whole lot of BS if you ask me!"

"Well I'm not asking! You're in or you're out Mick. This IS the future. We will no longer be a nation divided. With the push of only one political agenda, we will create..."

"Lemmings, Josh! Lemmings. A whole lotta lemmings trudging through a whole lotta BS! How can you have signed it off without mine and Sarah's agreement?"

"I didn't need it. We were never set up that way. And once I had told the board...come on Mick. Surely you can see the unity SMP will establish! You gotta see it!"

Mick hung his head down. When had his friend's ideals become so warped? Had they been so consumed with business that they had neglected friendship? He didn't know this person who was talking to him.

"And if me and Sarah don't agree?" Mick spoke calmly now. What other choice did he have?

"Well....it would pain me to say that we would have to cut all ties. Six months from now, SMP's likes will become currency. It will be how people live. This will help to create one idea amongst all. Six months after that, it will become compulsory."

Mick hadn't spoken to Josh since that conversation. He and Sarah had argued directly with the board and their investors to no avail. Everyone saw how it could profit them, but not how it could wound people. Six months later they packed up and headed home, relinquishing their involvement with SMP. Six months after that, they knew they had to go off the grid. So that same feeling of discomfort crept up Mick's spine, like icy finger tips on a cold winter's day.

"It will be okay," Sarah lightly touched Mick's shoulder as he stood in the doorway of the cabin.

"I thought you were worried," Mick replied softly.

"I was…I am. But we have to have hope. In the midst of this, we have to have hope. Otherwise what are we doing here? We may as well go back to the city and live under the rule of the new SMP."

"How do you do it? How do you…?" Mick rested his head on the bent frame of the door.

Sarah smiled tenderly and placed her head on Mick's shoulder. She never told him, but *he* was actually *her* anchor. Looking at him, she somehow knew, everything would be alright.

They had pottered around the cabin for the next few hours, making lunch for the children and playing games, until it was clear that the day was running away from them.

"Now I'm worried," Sarah said, after they had all eaten dinner.

"I'm going to look for them, before it is completely dark," Mick placed his hands in his pocket. As he was packing his back pack with supplies, he heard the rustling of leaves outside of the cabin. He looked over to Sarah. She had heard it too. Sarah quietly walked over to the children and held onto them. Suddenly, there was a tapping at the door.

"We know you're in there. We just want to ask a few questions. Don't try anything silly. The place is surrounded," the booming voice echoed throughout the cabin.

Mick and Sarah knew there was no way out. Escaping with the children would only mean that someone would get hurt. Their only option was to give themselves in and hope for the best. Mick slowly walked to the crooked door they had previously managed to close, and slightly opened it.

"We're a family of four enjoying a camping trip. Who are you and what can we help you with?" Mick knew full well who they were, but the less he gave away, the better.

"Government officials from the city," the man held up a badge high enough for Mick to see. "We're looking for a suspect. Can we check the cabin please? Just want to make sure everything is okay. A dangerous criminal is in this area and he could be anywhere."

Mick shot Sarah a look. Zen and Ellie.

"Erm… sure. Just me and my family and it's a small place." Mick held the door open revealing the tiny space. The official alongside two others who had been waiting behind him followed him in.

"A very… interesting place for you and your family to camp," the official noted after greeting Sarah and the children. The furniture was now pushed up to the side of one of the walls and blankets littered the floor.

"You know. We thought we could brave the tents, but changed our minds when we saw this cabin," Mick explained.

"I see," the official looked around the cabin skeptically. "I'm just going to do a few checks. Names please?"

Sarah looked at Mick. Mick felt the icy finger tips crawl up his spine and tighten around his neck.

"Is this really necessary? Obviously, the man you are looking for isn't here," Mick placed his hands in his pockets.

"Names please?" the official held Mick's stare.

"We don't want any trouble, we just want to continue with our camping trip. Or leave if there is a criminal in the area," Mick tried to stay calm and collected.

"Sir, I am going to have to take your name," the official held his gadget tightly in his hand, ready to search the database.

"Mike and Sarah Dorrset," Sarah said from the side of the room.

"Mike and Sarah Dorrset," the official repeated. "I've heard those names before."

The official began tapping on the screen of the tablet, with his face growing more and more confused as the seconds passed by.

"Definitely heard of your names before," he said again scratching his temple, "but you're not coming up."

"Could be this area. Very wooded," Mick suggested.

"Could very well be. Mick and Sarah Dorrset? One second," the official began frantically searching again. "Nope. I tried my name and my colleagues' names and they appeared. But there is no Mick and Sarah Dorrset. Let me see your ID."

Mick carefully took his ID out from his pocket and gave it to the official. Mick realized that the other two officials had their hands on their hips, ready for any trouble.

"Okay Mick Dorrset. This checks out. But I will need to bring you and your family in, as you are not on our system. You are now illegal citizens without signing up," the official held onto Mick's ID. The children will go with my colleague on the right. Your wife will need to go with my colleague on the left. And sir, you will need to come with me. If you refuse, we will have no choice but to use reasonable force."

Mick had expected immediate arrest, but then remembered that the SMP were subtle with their tactics. He told the children they would be fine if they went with the official and one of the officials took the children by the hand and led them outside. Sarah began to cry. Mick ran over to her to comfort her. The sudden movement surprised the official that had been waiting for Sarah to join him. He immediately pulled a steel object from his pocket and a loud bang erupted from the small item, followed by silence.

The first official immediately came running over to Mick and Sarah, who both now lay on top of each other on the floor. The official who fired the shot stood there, frozen to the spot, realising he had shot at unarmed civilians.

"Are you hurt?" the first official stood over the bodies.

Mick stood up rapidly in response, "What the hell?" Realising that Sarah was still lying on the floor, he called out for her. There was no response. Mick lay down beside her and touched her cold, clammy skin. "Sarah?"

Mick crouched over Sarah's body and continuously called out her name. He turned her body over to see that her left hand clung to the right side of her stomach. Blood streamed out of her side, as a solitary tear trailed down her face.

"Mick," she breathed softly, "I love you and I always will. You can do this."

"Don't talk Sarah. We need to get you help! Help her!" Mick screamed. By then, the first official had called for backup and more uniformed bodies marched into the room. Mick saw someone check over Sarah and before he knew it her body was being carried into one of their vehicles. The first official kept talking to Mick, telling him information he was sure was important, but he just kept seeing the man's mouth moving but no sound could be heard. Everyone seemed to be moving slowly around him and eventually someone carried him out to the cars parked outside. He realized he was being told that they would allow him to sit with his children for their journey into the city. The children, Mick thought. What was he going to say to them?

7

94 HOURS

"I...I...You can't be here."

"We have no choice." She looked in his eyes now. It was like she was travelling back in time. To when they would sit and talk until late, sharing each other's hopes and dreams. "There's a serial killer chasing us."

"Tom Miller? That's who we're looking for!"

"We gathered. I'm...we're still off the grid. But he tried to kill us." Zen then broke down into tears. She had been trying to hold everything for too long. Ellie placed her hand on Zen's shoulder.

"Zen. I'm so sorry. We have to catch him. Where did you see him?" Liam said sympathetically.

"It's...it's...," Zen struggled to get her words out.

"It's about a mile north," Ellie interjected. "An abandoned barn. But I wouldn't be surprised if he disappeared. We...Zen hit him over the head with a chair so my first guess is that he's looking for us."

Liam looked over at Zen and felt like all the breath within him disappeared. He had let her walk away. Out of his life and into this madness. He just wanted one more moment. One more moment to wrap her hair around his fingers. One more moment to feel her heart beat beating against his chest. One more moment...but all those moments had gone.

"I'm so sorry Zen," he pulled her close to him. One more moment.

"It's not safe for us here," Ellie looked around uncomfortably.

"Right. I've got a pick-up truck parked not too far from here. You can hide out in there. I'm going to tell the others where we can find Tom."

Liam led Ellie and Zen through the trees away from the eyes of the other officials. It wasn't a long walk to the truck. He helped them both up and placed a blanket over their heads. After about five minutes, Ellie and Zen could hear the sounds of boots plodding against the ground going deeper into the woods. They must have fallen asleep, because they were awoken by the rumble of the truck engine. In fear that they might get caught, Ellie and Zen kept their heads under the blanket until they heard the truck stop. The sudden slam of the truck door shook the vehicle. Ellie went to poke her head out from beneath the blanket, but Zen grabbed her hand. They couldn't afford to be running for their lives again. After fifteen minutes, the blanket was lifted slightly over their heads.

"I've got a plan. Don't say anything. You guys just have to stay here for another couple of hours. I'm going to put some supplies here. In about an hour or so you'll be able to reach in the bag and you won't be seen."

The truck was back on the road again and it was a few hours before the truck stopped.

"We're here. You can get out." Liam helped Ellie and Zen out of the truck.

"Where are we?" Ellie rubbed her eyes as they adjusted to the light.

"Just outside of the city. There are still a few areas not governed by the officials. It is safe for us to talk here," Zen saw Liam had changed out of his officials' uniform and had opted for a white t-shirt and jeans.

"How did you know where to find it?" Zen was confused about how a government official had known where to find the Rebels but hadn't done anything to capture them.

"I needed to know you were safe. I managed to find some of the camps. Asked around whilst posing as a Rebel. Nobody had heard of you. But I remembered where to find them, just in case you showed up there."

"Thank you, Liam. But what are you going to do?" Zen reached out for Liam's hand.

"I'm coming with you. I made the mistake of letting you go before. I'm not letting it happen again," Liam held Zen's hand.

Ellie started to pack the supplies in the truck and handed Liam and Zen a back pack each, "So what's the plan?"

"We need to find Mick and Sarah," Zen said determined.

"Mick and Sarah?" Liam looked at both Ellie and Zen.

"Yeah, the family who were in the cabin. We assumed that's why you were at the cabin. To take them away," Ellie replied.

"Oh," Liam slipped his hands into his pockets. "I'm really sorry. There was an incident. It happened before I arrived at the cabin. I heard they were taking the family because they were not showing up on the database. An official thought the husband and wife were going to attack and so shot at them. The wife was shot in the stomach. When I arrived at the cabin, I heard she had died on the way to the city."

Zen and Ellie stood in shock, listening to Liam relay what had been happening while they were escaping the clutches of a serial killer. Suddenly, Ellie burst out into tears.

"No. Not Sarah! Oh! And poor Mick! And the children!" Ellie placed her head into her hands and cried.

Zen looked up to the blue sky and walked away from Ellie and Liam, back down the path they had driven up. She placed her fingers on her temples and began rubbing her temples gently. After a few yards, she crouched down to the floor and cried. A few minutes later, she felt Liam place his hands around her shoulders.

"Zen? You okay?" Liam spoke softly.

"I...I...Sarah's gone," Zen sniffed.

"She is. I'm sorry. I just spoke to Ellie. She sounded like a really nice person."

"She was. We only knew her for a short time, but...the way she cared for us. Even when..." Zen looked up at Liam.

"What?"

"I confronted her. I confronted her and Mick quite aggressively. We found out they were the founders of SMP."

"What?" Liam looked at Zen in disbelief.

"Yeah. We were going to go the city. We were going to take down SMP," Zen looked into the distance, seemingly deep in thought. "We still have to. For Sarah. For Mick. For the children. For everyone whose lives have been robbed by SMP."

"Zen, come on," Liam was now holding Zen by her shoulders.

"I mean it Liam. It's one thing to force people away from their homes. A woman has lost her life. A husband has lost his wife and two children have lost their mom. SMP needs to be taken down Liam. Surely you see?"

"I said I would run away with you. But go back to SMP?"

"Liam. I'm not sure where 'we' stand, especially after the message you sent me, but this is something I definitely have to do."

"And me," Ellie was now standing behind them. "Like you said, for Sarah, Mick, the children and the rest of the world."

Liam sighed and put his hands by his side. "I'm not leaving you again Zen. I made that mistake before. Plus you need someone who knows the infrastructure of the SMP. I'll drive you. We better get going."

"Okay. So what's the plan?" Ellie asked.

"First, we need to find Mick. He will know how to take down SMP's programme. Then the rest should fall into place," Zen looked at Liam for reassurance.

"I know how we can get to Mick. But this is not going to be easy. You both will need to trust me. You sure you can do this?" Liam said.

Both Zen and Ellie nodded fervently in agreement.

Liam, Zen and Ellie ate and made their way back into the city. Zen and Ellie stayed hidden at the back of the truck to avoid any unfortunate encounters with the officials. Sounds of traffic and people flooded into the vehicle as Liam drove into the city. Zen and Ellie noticed that the quietness of the forest had now been exchanged for car horns blaring in the distance and engines roaring past them. Suddenly the noise stopped and a few moments later the vehicle came to a stop. The truck door opened and closed slowly and the sound of footsteps became louder.

"I'll be back in a minute," Zen and Ellie heard Liam speak over them.

Zen and Ellie waited patiently, staying as still as stone, scared to move not knowing where they actually were. About 15 minutes later, Liam pulled the blanket from over them.

"There's no one here, it's safe. And the security guard is taking a break," Liam helped Zen and Ellie out of the back and the truck.

Ellie noticed that in Liam's other hand was a huge black bag. Zen was too busy looking around their location. They were in an understory car park, with very few cars. Liam had parked in a shadowy area and the dim lights prevented them being seen any further.

"We're just below the main building. I decided to park in the old car park. No one parks here anymore since they created more modern parking areas. Here. I managed to grab some uniform for the officials. You both need to put these on," Liam handed them the uniform from the black bag.

Ellie made up her face as Liam placed the uniform in her hand.

"Come on. You need to trust me remember. You both can get changed in the truck. I left my uniform at the back of the truck, so I'll get changed there."

Once all three of them had changed into the officials' uniform, Liam led them into the back of the building. As they walked through the tall, glass doors, Zen and Ellie were astounded by what they saw. Government officials were casually walking around the foyer. Two tall white pillars stood in the middle of the room, with a receptionist desk positioned in the middle. Five elevators were on the other side of the foyer, which had been painted white all over. The lights inside the building were of huge contrast to the lights inside the car park. Ellie and Zen almost had to cover their eyes to prevent the lights from blinding them. Next to the elevators, there was a huge digital advertising screen.

"Here at SMP, we believe in people *living their best life. You can use your likes to create the life you have always wanted."*

"Pffft," Zen rolled her eyes. "How could you join them Liam?"

"It's a long story and one we don't have time for now. Come on."

Liam led Ellie and Zen to the first elevator, where there were a number of officials waiting. Zen overheard two officials in front of her discussing their likes.

"This job definitely has its advantages. The woman tried to give me an unlike but I just flashed my badge and her face immediately changed!"

'You better be careful. This uniform is not to push our own agenda but to push the company's agenda."

"It was a harmless reason. She thought I should have given her a larger tip. She's lucky I gave her a like in the first place."

Ding!

The elevator door opened and the officials waiting clambered into the small space. Liam pressed button 59, whilst the other officials pressed lower numbers. The elevator journey was silent until the other officials had exited out of the elevator.

"Okay, so we're going to floor 59. We really need to go to floor 65, but we need to not raise suspicion. Floor 65 is where they keep people who they have arrested," Liam said.

Once on floor 59, Liam led Ellie and Zen to the stairwell past dozens of people sitting on computers tapping away. The stairwell was dark and dingy and had evidently been neglected when everything else had been decorated.

"People rarely use the stairs," Liam said when he saw the look on Ellie and Zen's faces.

The three of them climbed the stairs until they reached floor 65. By time they got to that level, they were feeling tired and exhausted. Before Liam led them out of the stairwell, he shared his plan with Ellie and Zen.

"Okay. So the plan is to get to Mick. He will know what to do next. We'll have to find out which room he is being kept in and then say we need to give him his new identification. We'll take him back to this stairwell and discuss the plan. Easy peasy!" Liam looked at Ellie and Zen for their opinion.

"Sounds easy enough," Ellie said. Zen shrugged her shoulders in agreement.

They walked out of the stairwell into a corridor, which was just as gloomy as the stairwell. This floor seemed to have also experienced a level of neglect. The corridor led them into a circular room with a round desk in the middle and a number of rooms leading off. Two government officials stood at the round desk seemingly gossiping because they hadn't noticed their visitors.

"Ahem," Liam tried to get to their attention. "We're here to ID a prisoner… Mick Dorrset," Liam pretended to check his phone for details.

One of the officials, who seemed to be new to the job, went to immediately say where they would find the prisoner.

"Whoa, whoa, whoa. Remember we always check ID first," the other official pulled the inexperienced official back. "Sorry it's his first day. Can I get your ID?"

Liam handed his ID over to the official, who was now looking intently at Ellie and Zen.

"Ahhh. Female officials? What a rare sighting! Pretty as well, eh, Jack? This will probably be the first and last time you see such a thing," the official took Liam's ID without taking his eyes off Ellie and Zen. He then passed it over to the inexperienced official. "Take care of this will you, whilst I talk to our visitors."

Zen rolled her eyes when he turned to give the inexperienced official the ID and Liam looked at her as if to say, keep him busy.

"So, have you both been here before?" the official chatted away to Ellie and Zen, whilst Liam walked over to the official checking his ID.

"Everything okay?" Liam asked.

"Everything checks out sir," the official handed Liam his ID. "What about the other two?"

"Oh, they're with me. If your superior wasn't busy, he would tell you that one ID check is okay."

"Okay," the official eyes Liam suspiciously. "He's in room number 5."

"Thanks," Liam shook the official's hand and walked over to Zen and Ellie to try and rescue them.

"All done," Liam shook the other official's hand to break him from his conversation. "He checked my colleagues' IDs as well, so we're all clear."

"Great stuff. Pleasure to meet you ladies. Hope to see you again soon," the official shook Ellie's and Zen's hand after shaking Liam's.

Ellie and Zen followed Liam to room 5. Liam flashed his ID on the card reader outside the metal door and the door opened. Inside the small room, Mike sat on a bench with his head in his hands. As soon as the door opened, he looked up. His eyes were blood shot and his shoulders hung over in despair.

"I don't want to talk!" Mike's voice echoed around the room.

"Good luck," shouted the official from his desk. "This one is refusing to talk to anyone."

"We're here to ID you, sir," Liam said after looking over at the official.

"I don't want to receive an ID," Mike spat out. "I left because I didn't want an ID. Couldn't you just have left us alone." Mike's head fell back into his hands and his shoulders bobbed up and down as he began to sob.

Ellie and Zen felt his sadness and despair. Sarah was the love of his life. How will they get him out of his misery, let alone this room?

“Your file says you have two children, sir,” Ellie said putting on the ‘official’ talk. “You will have to make this sacrifice if you want to see them again.”

Mike suddenly stopped weeping and looked up at the three strangers in the room. “I want to see them. My children. I need to know if they are okay.”

“We can do that for you, if you come with us,” Ellie kept her voice stoic.

“Okay,” Mick stood up and looked past Liam, who was standing in front of Ellie and Zen. The sorrow that had covered his face had now been replaced by shock as he realized who he had been talking to. Ellie held her finger to her lips and signaled to Mick to follow them.

Mick walked out of the room, following Liam, Zen and Ellie.

“No cuffs?” the official shouted out to them as they walked into the corridor.

“His file says he’s harmless,” Liam shouted back. “Besides there’s enough of us to take him down if necessary.”

Nobody spoke after that until they entered the stairwell.

“I can’t believe we did it,” Liam was evidently relieved, as he ran his right hand through his hair and leant against the wall.

Mick took a seat on the first descending step and placed his head his hands. “We made it. Sarah didn’t.”

Zen and Ellie walked towards Mick and placed their hands on his shoulders.

"We're so sorry," Ellie spoke softly. She was lost for words.

"What happened?" Zen mirrored Ellie's tone.

"They shot her. Thought we were going to retaliate…and they shot her," Mick began sobbing. No one spoke for another five minutes.

"Mick. We're really sorry… but we came to stop this problem. To stop the SMP from ruining people's lives," Liam walked over to where Mick was sitting.

Mick stood up abruptly, "You're right! Sarah would want us to do this. Then…then when we've destroyed this God-forsaken company, we need to find my kids!" Mick suddenly began marching down the dark stair well. Presuming he knew where he was going, the others followed in silence.

8

118 HOURS

It didn't take them long to reach floor 50, which had the room that held the SMP database. Before they left the stairwell, Mick shared with the group what his plans were.

"So before I left, I was worried that those who were running SMP may try and do something dangerous with the company. Thinking that the time may arise where I would have to do something about it, I coped some of the codes from SMP onto a USB. These codes can destroy the whole thing. We just have to get into the room," Mick dug into his pocket and held out the USB for everyone to see. "The room will possibly have a few guards and chances are someone out there will recognize me. Therefore, this is where I have to leave you. You just have to find the central computer, put the USB and download the codes. It sounds easy but," Mick began to rub his forehead, "but, you will need to type in a security code to start the process. You will also need ID to gain access into the room."

"I like how you left the hardest part until the end," Ellie wrapper her hair around her hands.

"Okay so not easy at all. If you get access, it will be using one of the guards' ID. While you do that, I will look for my children," Mick gave the USB to Liam.

"So that's it? There's no other way for us to get into the room?" Zen gave Mick a look of bewilderment.

"Well, we intended to sit down and plan this out properly Zen. But look at the situation we are in. Time is of the essence here, and I am afraid that we are just going to have to act," Mick said.

"We can do this. We made it this far," Ellie placed her hand on Zen's shoulder. "Let's at least take a moment to think."

Everyone stood in silence, contemplating their next move. After about five minutes, Liam cried out that he had come up with an idea. He shared his idea and in response he saw heads nodding excitedly in agreement. When Liam had finished sharing the idea, Mick said his goodbyes to the group and carried on his descent down the stairwell.

"And then there were three," Ellie said as she looked towards the entrance to the corridor.

"Ready?" Liam asked.

"As we'll ever be," Zen replied.

Zen, Ellie and Liam walked out towards the corridor and opened the door into a huge white room. The empty room was bare except for two guards on the other side guarding a door. As soon as they saw the three strangers approach them, their hands moved towards the weapons resting on their hips.

"Changeover is in another two hours," said one of the guards.

"And there doesn't need to be three of you," said the other.

"So you better explain yourself quickly," said the first guard.

Liam underestimated how hard this was going to be. He held out his badge towards the guards.

"Nothing like that - Don't worry. Hands off the weapons. We're just doing our checks and making sure everyone's in their positions," Liam spoke confidently.

"Oh, okay. Well we're both accounted …" the first guard began to say.

"Radioing in all armed guards. You are needed on the 65th floor. There has been an attempt to break out one of our prisoners," the crackled voice came from one of the guard's radios.

Both of the guards looked at each, uncertain of leaving their posts.

"I know we don't have any weapons but we can hold the fort until you come back. The last thing you want is for someone to question why you were just standing here doing nothing. And if anything there's three of us, so it should be okay," Liam's convincing tone seemed to be persuading the guards as they edged further away from the locked door.

"Okay. We'll be ten minutes. Any suspicious activity, make sure you radio someone in," the first guard spoke as he led the second guard back to the corridor.

When Liam was sure they had definitely gone, he typed in the code Mick had given him into the keypad. A red light flashed back at him. Ellie pushed the door but the door was locked.

"They must have changed it when Mick left," Liam banged the keypad.

"I have an idea," Zen walked over to the fire alarm in the corner of the room. "In case of a fire, all doors are unlocked." Zen punched through the safety glass and the loud, blaring noise erupted from the ceiling.

"Can all personnel please report to the fire assembly points?"

Ellie pushed the door again. Locked.

"Okay. So not all doors," Zen tried to shout over the alarm.

"What about this?" Ellie walked over to the corner of the room and picked up a fire extinguisher.

"There's not really a fire," Liam shouted.

Ellie raised her eyebrow and then lifted the fire extinguisher over her head. As she brought it down, she made sure the extinguisher collided with the lock on the door.

Once they were in the room, they looked for the main computer. All around the room, there were monitors displaying various codes.

"Why is this room left empty? Don't people need to be manning these computers?" Ellie asked.

Zen placed the USB into what appeared to be the main computer and waited for the programme to load up. Suddenly a dialogue box popped up on the screen, asking Zen if she wanted to run the programme. When asked to do so, she typed in the password, S-A-R-A-H and then waited. A number of incomprehensible words and phrases appeared on the screen and then the words, 'Everything will be deleted. Are you sure?' took its place.

"Are you really sure Zen?" a voice said from the doorway.

Zen turned around to see a man standing in the doorway, with three guards standing behind him.

"How do you know who I am?" Zen asked.

"Ahhh from your precious Liam. Hello Liam. Didn't take you long to switch sides. And in answer to your question Zen, you can learn a lot from a person's profile. Their thoughts. Their feelings. Their love interests," the man spoke sternly.

"Who are you?" Ellie asked.

"The question is, what are you three doing in here? A place you shouldn't be? Has Liam told you yet why he joined us Zen?" the man looked from Liam to Zen.

"That's enough Mr. Davis. We're just here to do something that should have been done years ago," Liam stepped in front of Zen and Ellie.

"No need for pleasantries now that we are in this predicament. You can call me Josh, creator of the SMP," Josh spat out.

"That's where you are wrong. This was a dream belonging to Mick and Sarah," Ellie shouted angrily.

"Mick and Sarah? A dream? Ha! They wouldn't understand a vision even if it had millions of followers. At some point we had to move on without them," Josh's eyes were filled with fury.

"And create this? People have tried to fight against this dictatorship and feeling that they can't win they have gone into hiding. Families have been broken and lives have been lost!" Zen yelled, her hand steadily holding onto the mouse of the computer.

"I guess Mick and Sarah have been feeding you their lies. I guess they haven't told you what good SMP have done. Well Liam, your turn to tell the truth. Why did you become an SMP official?" Josh stared at Liam waiting for an answer.

Liam looked uneasily from Josh to Zen, not wanting to share this secret with her.

"Fine! Liam here joined us because he needed to pay for his heart defect. Your precious Liam found out that he had a heart defect and needed to gain enough likes to pay for his operation. Where best to come to, than SMP?" Josh smiled menacingly.

"I'm sorry," Liam whispered to Zen.

"Why didn't you tell me?" Zen began to cry.

"Oh, she's upset. Well missy, if you delete SMP, you would have gotten rid of everything Liam has worked for. Who will pay for his precious operation then? The whole system will crash," Josh waited as his message sunk in. "Or, you could leave now, and we won't say a word. Liam here can get his operation, and everyone can live happily ever after."

Zen looked back at the computer, blinded by her tears. She could hardly make out the message on the screen, but saw the cursor hovered over the word 'Yes'.

"So, what is it, Zen? Are you going to click?"

The story continues…

and you can decide what happens next.

Does Zen click?

Does she save Liam's life?

Write your version of what you think should happen in the next part of the story, post it on Instagram and tag @_click_story_.

Follow @_click_story_ on Instagram, where you can access the latest updates on the book.

ABOUT THE AUTHOR

Antonique Wickham was born in Germany but raised in Birmingham, England. From a young age, she has always had a love for writing, whether it was writing poetry or creating her own books. This transpired into her creating a blog for her to further experiment with the art of words. She now teaches as well as writing short stories to further explore the power of putting pen to paper.

Printed in Great Britain
by Amazon